Text copyright © Anthony Masters 1997
Illustrations copyright © Alan Marks 1997

First published in Great Britain in 1997
by Macdonald Young Books

Re-issued in 2008 by Wayland

Printed and bound in China

British Library Cataloguing in Publication Data available

ISBN 978 0 7502 5415 1

Wayland is a division of Hachette Children's Books,
an Hachette Livre UK Company
www.hachettelivre.co.uk

The Haunted Lighthouse

Anthony Marks

Illustrated by Alan Marks

WAYLAND

Chapter One

The seals crowded the rock below Seal Rock Lighthouse. They gazed up at Philip who stared back in amazement. He had never seen so many, their dark skins glistening, their eyes watching him closely.

A winter storm was brewing. The sky was black and the waves were getting bigger, pounding on the reef that stretched out to sea like a row of sharp teeth.

He was standing in the top chamber where the light used to revolve, warning ships off the rocks with its bright white beam. But now that the big lamp had been shut down, the lighthouse had become a museum.

Philip and his father had moved there a month ago when his father had become curator. Philip's grandfather had been the last of the lighthouse keepers, but he had drowned whilst out fishing in his boat years before Philip was born. Philip often thought about him, wondering what his life must have been like.

Philip didn't like living at the lighthouse. He was lonely without his friends and felt uneasy being so close to the sea. It was spooky.

The biggest seal was on the very top of the rock now. His eyes seemed to be boring straight into Philip's. Philip felt uncomfortable and wondered why. Then he remembered how local people believed that inside the seals were the souls of the drowned.

Philip told himself the legend was just a made-up story. But the idea wouldn't go away and his uneasiness increased.

Lightning split the sky in a series of jagged flashes, and then a growl of thunder came from far out to sea. In the eerie silence that followed, Philip heard the sound of his father's footsteps ringing out on the spiral staircase that led to the top chamber.

Gasping for breath, Philip's father reached the top chamber, but when he caught sight of the seals he looked as scared as Philip. "I've never seen so many before."

"Neither have I," said Philip. "What are they all doing there?"

"It's just like your grandad used to say…" His father hesitated.

"What did he say, Dad?" Philip asked irritably, wondering why his father hadn't finished what he was saying.

"When the seals gather on Seal Rock, there'll be a shipwreck," he replied reluctantly and then added, "It's just an old story, of course."

They both gazed down at the rock that crouched under the lighthouse. The thunder growled again and the lightning lit the sky, making the seals look white and ghostly.

Chapter Two

Philip first heard the footsteps on the stairs while he was reading in bed. He sat up and listened. What was Dad doing, going up to the chamber again?

Then to his surprise, his father opened the door and came into the bedroom. So he wasn't on the stairs after all.

But someone was. Philip could hear pounding feet on the staircase above that began to break into a run. He could also hear the gasping of breath, and anxious mutterings.

"Can't you hear those footsteps, Dad?" Philip was confused.

"What footsteps?" His father listened and then shrugged. "It's the storm. Hailstones most likely."

"They're on the staircase. Going up."
Philip was really scared now.

"I can't hear anything, it's just the
storm." With that, his father said
goodnight and went out. As he did so, the
footsteps stopped as suddenly as they had
begun. Philip was left wondering if he
had imagined what he had
heard. Maybe he was
feverish.

Philip tried to sleep but only managed to doze uneasily.

Suddenly he sat bolt upright, shivering and shaking all over. He could hear the footsteps again. This time they were even louder and more urgent than before and the rasping of breath was much closer.

Philip nervously got up and ran down the staircase, only to find his father reading a paper in the living room.

"Can't you sleep?" his father asked crossly.

"I just wanted a glass of water," snapped Philip. If only they were back home and not living in this creepy lighthouse, he would be able to sleep.

Whilst he was in the kitchen, Philip listened carefully but could only hear the booming of the sea. Reluctantly, he went back to bed again.

Chapter Three

Philip's head was too full of footsteps and thunder and homesickness to try to sleep again. The flashes of lightning made his furniture look as if it had suddenly been painted white.

Eventually Philip drifted off into another light doze from which he soon woke abruptly, hearing the footsteps yet again. This time the gasping seemed even nearer than before.

She'll be on the rocks if she doesn't change course. The strange voice rang inside his mind.

Philip was terrified. What was happening
to him now? Had he made the words up?
Imagined them? He sat up in bed, his
heart racing. Tiptoeing fearfully to his
bedroom door he opened it slowly.
Someone was running up the spiral
staircase, their footsteps
hammering the
iron rungs.

The figure was misty, shadowy, hardly there at all. Then the shape became more solid and Philip could see a tall man wearing a cap and a thick sweater. He had a white beard and a straggling moustache, and Philip could even see the sweat streaming down his face.

The figure began to fade away, and Philip shook with fear. What was going on? He knew he had to find out.

Philip ran towards the staircase and then more slowly and cautiously began to climb to the light chamber at the top. It was a long way up and the higher he got, the colder he became.

Halfway up he stopped, too scared to continue. He clung to the rail as hard as he could, shivering violently, as if he were under the ice of a frozen lake. Gradually the feeling passed, and he began to climb again.

Chapter Four

Somehow, Philip forced himself on, and
the faster he climbed the warmer he began
to feel. But when he reached the top the
cold feeling came back much more
strongly and Philip found it hard to catch
his breath. He was freezing again now and
his icy fingers fumbled with the latch. At
last he managed to open the door.

The light chamber was filled with a
floating fog and he could hardly see
anything. Gradually it cleared, and Philip
could make out the shimmering figure of
the man in the sweater gazing out into the
storm. He was wearing
a cap that looked
exactly like the
keeper's cap in the
museum display.

Still standing by the door, not daring to move, Philip could just see out through the huge glass windows. The seals were lying on the rock in the boiling surf, but the big seal he had noticed earlier was no longer there.

The rain was lashing down and the wind was wailing and shrieking. Philip peered into the distance, trying to see what the keeper was staring at.

Then, dimly glowing through the driving rain he could just make out a ship's lights, and he remembered the voice that had so frighteningly entered his mind.

She'll be on the rocks if she doesn't change course.

Right now the ship was heading straight for the reef.

Slowly turning away from the windows, the keeper began to drift towards the great lamp that had once revolved, warning ships about the dangerous rocks.

Philip knew he couldn't even begin to explain that the light was no longer working, so he began to run back down the spiral staircase for help.

Chapter Five

Philip took a couple of minutes getting his sleepy father to understand that there was a ship heading for the rocks. He didn't dare tell him about the ghostly figure upstairs.

Philip's father leapt out of bed and pulled open the curtains. Sure enough, the ship's lights were brighter and she was even nearer the cruel black rocks that were about to rip her open.

"That ship's in the wrong channel!" shouted Philip's father. "She'll hit the rocks."

Philip shouted back above the crashing thunder, "We'll have to phone the coastguards."

His father gazed anxiously out of the window, knowing they would arrive too late. "Yes, but we need to warn the ship now," he yelled, pulling a coat over his pyjamas. "Come on, we'll use the car headlights. Maybe the captain will see the high beam."

They quickly phoned the coastguard. Then Philip's father backed the car out of the garage and screeched it up to the headland with the headlights full on. Philip had never seen him drive so fast as the old car rocked about on the bumpy track that wound over the cliffs.

For a dreadful moment Philip thought they were going over the edge as the car skidded while his father fought to control the wheel. The car just missed going over the drop and for a few terrifying seconds Philip saw the beach below.

At the last minute, his father straightened the car and screamed to a muddy, squelching stop. Then he inched forwards, the headlights like huge eyes staring out into the storm.

But the rain was too heavy and the beam too dim to warn the ship. Philip could just make out the name on her side. *Pride of Portsmouth.*

"There's nothing else we can do," yelled his father above the storm. "Let's go back, Phil. It's no use."

Chapter Six

Reluctantly, Dad turned the car round and skidded down the track to the lighthouse. He stopped the car and ran towards the door. "I'll see what the coastguards are doing," he shouted.

When his father had gone inside, Philip turned to take one last look at the doomed ship. Then, to his amazement, he saw the waves were suddenly bathed in brilliant white light. Looking up, Philip realised it came from the lighthouse. This was impossible. It just couldn't be happening. None of the equipment worked. So how could the light shine out like this?

Philip ran back up the spiral staircase, going as fast as he dared.

When he arrived at the top, Philip felt the intense cold again and could smell brine and seaweed. Then he saw the same ghostly figure tending the light.

The ship's turning back, came the keeper's voice in Philip's mind.

I got here in time.

He was right. The *Pride of Portsmouth*
was turning, slowly heading back out to
sea, leaving the jagged line of foam-
covered rocks behind.

"Who are you?" whispered Philip but
there was no reply. *Who are you?* Philip
asked again, now speaking silently, in his
mind. This time the keeper seemed to
hear him.

He began to move towards Philip without making a sound, his eyes glowing like fog-lamps, his breath so cold that it felt like a blast of frosty air.

Philip backed away, but still the keeper walked on, arms outstretched as if he were searching for someone. There was something weird about his fingers.

They were growing dark fur. Philip could see it sprouting out of the old flesh.

Then he turned away and returned to the lamp, focusing the beam downwards towards the sea. The waiting seals were lit up by the bright light and Philip could see there was a vacant space on the highest part of the rock. Slowly the keeper began to walk towards the window.

His shape was shimmering again and
Philip was suddenly more afraid than
he'd ever been before. Something was
happening to the keeper. The rest of
his body seemed to be growing dark fur
as well.

Who are *you*? Despite his fear, Philip
tried to make contact again.

Chapter Seven

The figure gazed intently at Philip.

Suddenly he remembered an old photograph his father had once shown him. The ghostly figure's beard and moustache were instantly familiar.

Philip knew he was gazing into the eyes of his grandfather.

The old man turned away and strode on, walking through the glass, travelling down the lamp's beam, the wind sweeping through his fur.

The circular room was empty now. Yet the lamp was still projecting its beam. Philip ran to the window. For a moment he could see the lashing spray, the boiling surface of the angry sea that pounded the rocks. Then Philip hit the glass and fell back, winded. Struggling slowly to his feet he gazed out at the sea.

The waves parted for an instant as the big seal slid on to the rock to join its companions. Then, with a thundering roar, the surf came up again and the light went out.

Dimly, Philip could just make out the black hulk of the *Pride of Portsmouth* as she sailed safely back into the main channel.

Still shaking, Philip stared down at the
foaming rock. The big seal was back and
gazing up at him steadily.

Suddenly Philip didn't fear the sea any
more. He knew he shared a secret with his
grandfather now. In fact, for the first time,
Philip felt he belonged here.

As he heard his father's footsteps on the spiral staircase, Philip picked up his grandfather's cap which was lying on the floor. The inside was wet and smelt of seaweed. Hurriedly, he put it in his pocket, just as his bewildered father reached the top chamber.

DARE TO BE SCARED!

Are you brave enough to try more titles in the Tremors series?
They're guaranteed to chill your spine…

The Ghost Bus by Anthony Masters
When Jack and Tina catch a late bus home from school, they realise that something is wrong. This bus is very old-fashioned, but what really gives them a fright is the passengers – they can see right through them! They're on a ghost bus, a ghost bus with a mission…

The Headmaster's Ghost by Sam Godwin
It's the school trip to Mortimer Hall. Adam and Melissa decide to scare Danny senseless by telling him the story of the evil headmaster's ghost who haunts the house. Danny is determined to show he isn't scared. But does his detemination bring him more than he bargained for…?

Terror in the Attic by Barbara Mitchelhill
A lodger has rented the attic in Craig and Kelly's house, but there is something odd about him. Why does he always dress in black? What is in his leather bag? Desperate to solve the mystery of this stranger they decide to explore the attic. But does their curiosity get the better of them…?

Ghost on the Landing by Eleanor Allen
It's the curse of the top landing. If any boy bullies a girl there, she can call for REVENGE. Louise almost starts to believe the ghostly tale she invents to stop Jack bullying her. There's certainly more moving up there than just ancient dust…

Tremors are available from your local bookshop or can be ordered direct from the publishers. For more information about Tremors write to: *The Sales Department, Hachette Children's Books, 338 Euston Road, London NW1 3BH.*